Amitava Nag

AF205008

Radha

a collection of ten Indian short stories

JustFiction Edition

Impressum/Imprint (nur für Deutschland/only for Germany)
Bibliografische Information der Deutschen Nationalbibliothek: Die Deutsche Nationalbibliothek verzeichnet diese Publikation in der Deutschen Nationalbibliografie; detaillierte bibliografische Daten sind im Internet über http://dnb.d-nb.de abrufbar.
Alle in diesem Buch genannten Marken und Produktnamen unterliegen warenzeichen-, marken- oder patentrechtlichem Schutz bzw. sind Warenzeichen oder eingetragene Warenzeichen der jeweiligen Inhaber. Die Wiedergabe von Marken, Produktnamen, Gebrauchsnamen, Handelsnamen, Warenbezeichnungen u.s.w. in diesem Werk berechtigt auch ohne besondere Kennzeichnung nicht zu der Annahme, dass solche Namen im Sinne der Warenzeichen- und Markenschutzgesetzgebung als frei zu betrachten wären und daher von jedermann benutzt werden dürften.

Coverbild: www.ingimage.com

Verlag: JustFiction! Edition ist ein Imprint der
LAP LAMBERT Academic Publishing GmbH & Co. KG
Heinrich-Böcking-Str. 6-8, 66121 Saarbrücken, Deutschland
Telefon +49 681 37 20 310, Telefax +49 681 37 20 310-9
Email: info@justfiction-edition.com

Herstellung in Deutschland:
Schaltungsdienst Lange o.H.G., Berlin
Books on Demand GmbH, Norderstedt
Reha GmbH, Saarbrücken
Amazon Distribution GmbH, Leipzig
ISBN: 978-3-8454-4524-3

Imprint (only for USA, GB)
Bibliographic information published by the Deutsche Nationalbibliothek: The Deutsche Nationalbibliothek lists this publication in the Deutsche Nationalbibliografie; detailed bibliographic data are available in the Internet at http://dnb.d-nb.de.
Any brand names and product names mentioned in this book are subject to trademark, brand or patent protection and are trademarks or registered trademarks of their respective holders. The use of brand names, product names, common names, trade names, product descriptions etc. even without a particular marking in this works is in no way to be construed to mean that such names may be regarded as unrestricted in respect of trademark and brand protection legislation and could thus be used by anyone.

Cover image: www.ingimage.com

Publisher: JustFiction! Edition
is an imprint of the publishing house
LAP LAMBERT Academic Publishing GmbH & Co. KG
Heinrich-Böcking-Str. 6-8, 66121 Saarbrücken, Germany
Phone +49 681 37 20 310, Fax +49 681 37 20 310-9
Email: info@justfiction-edition.com

Printed in the U.S.A.
Printed in the U.K. by (see last page)
ISBN: 978-3-8454-4524-3

Amitava Nag

Radha

Table of Contents

Radha

Radha used to love us most – me and *bhai*, my brother. In our joint family of our *kakas* (father's younger brothers)and *jethus* (father's elder brothers) we never really knew who Radha was. Probably she was the orphan daughter of one of my dead uncle. Probably, yes, we were never very sure. It was difficult – in a flock of cousins it took ages before I knew for sure that Rakhi is my own sister and Ranjan-*da* is my cousin. So we grew up thus in a huddle, wetting beds and listening to the moaning of elders. And we had Radha who always kept the best pickle for us, the best twig which she found in her afternoon adventures in the scarce bush at the far end of the garden. We had a big house. We had so many people that we had none to look after us. Radha, was our mentor.

Yet, she was despised by *Ma* and *Kakimas* (my aunties).

'Uff, she is a burden. God knows why her parents left this mad girl on us. See, how they shrugged off their responsibilities!'- *Ma* used to shout.

'Why do you always say Radha is mad? She gives us marbles, *Ma* and also she prepares food for Rukmini'.

'Who is this Rukmini?'- *Ma* fumes.

'Rukmini, you don't know, the squirrel in our mango tree'.

'Oh this is what you do all afternoon. No studies? Huh' – *Ma* slams her hand at me. I frisk away and run.

'Remember, this girl wont leave you, she will eat you and your *bhai*'.

'Will you eat us Radha? *Ma* told me'. I was nervous.

'I don't know Sona. They all tell me that I am witch. I ate my parents and now..' She was pensive, and suddenly,

'But I will not leave anyone who dares to touch you, see what they have done, to take you two away' - Radha suddenly took off her blouse and we saw her black back marked with bruises.

'Touch them' - she ordered? I was afraid. I was not sure if I reached puberty, *bhai* even less. And we have been growing up in a gang hearing about masturbation and eyeing girls' bosoms. Suddenly Radha hit me as I fell down and she put her feet on my chest.

'See I am Ma Kali – don't you dare to disobey' – she started laughing , she bends over as she laughed and then she cried and cried. We ran and we shivered. That night I ejaculated and Radha had high fever, *Baba* told.

Radha's incarnation of Goddess Kali was however not kept secret. Banshi of the higher class took me by collar,

'Hey, heard that dusky girl of your house is putting up Kali show?' he winked. I was unsure and he hit me. They were in a group, circling me and jibing.

'Radha, they told bad things in your name' I objected to her.

'Leave them Sona, they are like that only, don't you know?' Then one Sunday afternoon we were playing marbles at this side when suddenly *bhai* told –

'Look, Banshi and his friends there, near the mango tree'. They were teasing Radha –

'Eh..you Kali? Show us that you are Kali. How do you pee? Can you pee while standing? Like us?' They mocked and laughed. And in that blazing trace of the last straws from the Sun, Radha took her dress off and stood there – as the naked Goddess Kali. I was frightened. There was something in the air, some premonition – it was *Baba* and *Chhoto Kaka* (my youngest uncle). Hearing them Banshi fled with his group. *Baba* started rebuking Radha and they dragged her inside. *Ma* and others beat her up,

'You are getting old Radha. What type of decency have you learnt? You sex maniac' – *Ma* shouted. We were shivering in tension, if something happens to Radha who will be our playmate? Radha stayed still in a mess with high fever for few days. We used to go to her room stealthily

'Why do you do things that elders don't approve Radha?', *bhai* asked. She winked,

'There is no fun in obeying, kids. Grow up!'

The last time Radha was beaten up so badly was when she missed her periods. She didn't tell anyone, but who can escape *Ma*'s hawkish eyes? She gnarled us

'Speak out. You two must be knowing'.

'No, *Ma*. Seriously No'. Then she took up with Radha. My other aunties joined in venting authority. Radha didn't say anything. She didn't tell them a single word, not the name who made her pregnant, not even *Chhoto Kaka*'s !

That night Radha was hospitalized. *Ma* slapped us and told,

'If anyone asks, tell that she fell from the tree'. We were terrified. Is Radha really a witch? We weren't sure. But by then we knew that virgin girls cannot become pregnant. So utter confusion. I asked *Chhoto Kaka*, can't virginity be cured? *Chhoto Kaka* gave a vacant smile.

Since then Radha's room was locked up. We grew up from feeble boys to fat men believing it was a curse room. Only when my cousin came back from her in-laws' house permanently with her son, *Chhoto Kaka* left his room for them and moved to Radha's. He had retired by then. Every eclipse, *Chhoto Kaka* cries and screams in the courtyard, he doesn't want to stay in; he doesn't want to wear clothes.

ENDNOTE : There are several Bengali (Indian) names of relationships which have been used here. They have also been defined in the content itself.

18th June

1

He lays exasperated. His computer room is dim lit and as he stretched his naked legs on the chair, he looks up to see Che looking from the poster. Are the eyes on him, or they are turned to the side in disgust? Suddenly he felt cold, and he reached for his pajamas.

> He is a good boy, proverbially. He was good in studies. He was liked by the aunties of the apartment where he lived. His notes were in demand – to most, he was the ideal Indian boy. And he always enjoyed being 'good', respecting elders and looking for the dream job – being an engineer.

As the strings of the sitar filled the room he leaned back. And closed his eyes.

> Ravishankar deliberated on Misra Pilu and he knew he is getting the feeling of being engulfed with a sense of purposelessness. As the chords flowed from one corner to the other, his heart leapt and he could sense it lurking in front of him.

- *'What you want?', he is tired.*
- *'An answer' came the reply*
- *'Which question?' he feels dejected*
- *'How long I will linger?'*
- *'I don't know, leave me. But don't leave me. I am afraid', he was all tears.*
- *'Take your time. There is no shame in admitting fear. I will ask again'.*

He gets up from a slumber which lasted many years, as if. And he shrugged off. Where does the road lead to, he wonders? Today's was the best. She must be very good orally, he thought. He could almost sense his tongue running the length of her neck on her eve's apple. He bites, this is the golden tool which gives me so much please, he feels.

And then he gets up in a flash and slams the door behind.

2

She was looking at her in the mirror in the bathroom. The shower overhead was old and the trickle from its half-choked face found its path in the mystic curves of her. She is reaching menopause and her breasts her pensive about it. She heaves a sigh and holds her left nipple up and looks at the mirror – 'wakeup sleeping queen', she murmurs.

She gets late for office and needs to hurry up but she drags herself to a cozy siesta. There is no one to track her the whole day, no one to pamper. The left-over of the last night are still rotting in the refrigerator – as if they were her self, slowly poisoned by a cool numbness.

'What did go wrong?' she thinks. She finds none. But not all is okay. She knows that even, a realization she wanted to succumb to her desires. The colleague of the same department is taking interest. She can read it in his eyes. She had been reading men's eyes since she was in the convent in the mountains.

She opens her collection of men eyes – a scrapbook her husband found obnoxious. 'Look at me, you all, am I getting old?', she bares her for them. She can feel the eyes running up and down her chest, her deep navel and even down. Her navel was such a craze amongst her friends, she remembered – this is the one which remained the same through plunders and sorrows. She knew she is melancholic.

3

He cannot concentrate in his studies. He is expecting a birthday wish from his grandpa – he always wishes first.

He opens up his chat window - 'How many men praised your eyes?', he asks. She tries to recall, but can't. That's her 'Best Feature' that she has mentioned in her Orkut profile. He felt he has seen the eyes, they were so familiar. Just the eyes. The look. The haunted black-hole he wished he could dive in it.

- *'My mom left my dad and me when I was three. My dad used to beat her up', he confessed.*
- *'Why? What was her fault?' she would enquire.*
- *'Nothing as such. He was in love with other women', he justifies.*
- *'Then why didn't she take you with her. She didn't love you that means?' she was reasoning.*
- *'NOOOOOO', he yells.*

He was never sure why her mom left him. There are no photos of her in their house. He heard his mom loved someone else. He didn't accept it. His dad was no saint. But he imagined many such dialogues, soliloquies withered with time.

At school, when Rakesh's mom died of cancer, he cried. If his mom would have died thus, it could have been so respectful, he thought. And then a sense of guilt engulfed him. He will find her one day, he thought. But he never knew, how?

4

He is still on the other side. Lurid yet defenseless, manly yet childish. She is bored with 'mature' men. He is better. She enjoys this mystic virtual conversation. But he is young and demanding, obvious. Is she getting old? She feels she is not that reciprocative. She doesn't like the virtual thing always. Isn't she bored with the actual as well, she reflects.

It is 4:05 in the morning, 18th June. She suddenly remembers, twenty years back she gave birth to her only son this very moment. She caresses her stretch marks in fond memories. He gave him so much pain in labour. She cried and cried and then so much peace, so much happiness. The first rays of the son lengthened on his face, and she named him Pratyush, the dawn.

What is she doing now. For all these twenty years? What is Pratyush doing? She sobbed and sobbed. Its raining outside. She closed her laptop. Goodbye my virtual friend. Goodbye.

Atleast today, leave me alone. Today is my son's twentieth birthday. He is a man. My man.

The four letter word

I

Lata gasps her breath. She sees him enter. The dance floor bursts. Ravi is a macho. He is dashing, handsome. Lata is cute, small. It's party time now. They completed a year. The college feels cozy. Old friends have withered. New acquaintances blossomed radiant. Lata loves Ravi, madly. He started returning favours. This is the event.

- Hi sweetie, been long?
- Nope. Waiting for you

Ravi grabs Lata's waist. Draws her even close. She smells after shave. She feels so intoxicated. Ravi knows to handle. Girls, liquor and money. The music is deafening. Mosaic lights throw shadows. And the two dance. She matches her man. He tires his prey.

The lights go off. It's late and over. Lata doesn't stop crying. Ravi gets bored increasingly. He just dumps girls. But Lata is different. He sensed her urge. To satisfy her man. She is petite wild. Lata trembles in despair. She is in love. Deeper than virginal woes.

- Lets leave now sweetie
- Please don't leave me

- What nonsense you speak
- I can't stay alone
- Don't be a fool
- I love you Ravi
- I love you too
- Will you marry me?

Ravi is not sure. It's too much commitment. He is quite young. His family is rich. Lata will be misfit. Lata clasps his hands. She can't waive now. Her mother and sisters. Their hope on her. A family of women. She falters, and cries.

Ravi feels irritated now. He needs a bath. To wash off memories.

II

Old rivalry breeds hatred. Jai knows pretty well. Dimple is the bimbo. Jai's hunger is insatiable. Dimple ignores him always. She is after Ravi. Ravi is too strong. His father has influences. That frustrates even more. Jai spoke with Dimple. Tried to convince her. But she is adamant. Girls are fools, always. Jai is pretty sure.

The party was bore. Dimple had a fracture. She was not there. Bad luck to losers. Ravi was with Lata. This makes Jai angry. How easily they change.

Like changing clothes daily. Jai feels like fighting. He then restrains himself. There is no use.

The mobile camera blinked. The couple was intimate. Jai was taken aback. His idea was wrong. Lata wasn't that innocent. Few pegs of vodka. Jai went overboard instantly. Justice has denied him. Streaks of revenge resurface.

The pics are beads. They stitch up stories. Jai is so happy. He strikes a plan.

The mail server shivers. MMS clips fly off. Dimple can't believe this. She was so blind. She calls it quits.

No one knew details. None wanted to even. They relished the contents.

III

Vibgyor is her favourite. Their town paints rainbows. Will she ever return? The shame is manifold. She can't think anymore. Ravi has behaved awkward. How can he escape? She is discussed everywhere. Inside college, even outside. She can't stand this.

Then she remembers colours. She loved to draw. Rain drops and lillies. Ages she didn't draw. Till Ravi's birthday card. She can see colours. Everywhere, even in death. What is death's colour? To her it's white. White is always sacred. Death is freedom too. Her father committed suicide. He couldn't feed them. Her father wore white.

The night grows still. Only the dogs bark. The lampposts stare alone. She gets her up. The white pad glares. She will deflower it. Who will be responsible? She pens her name. Her own name – Lata.

Outside, the night sleeps. Inside the turmoil heightens. She holds back breath. The fragrance of life. Gone in one week? Is life so cheap? So full of threats? So dull yet arrogant? She feels like quitting.

She calls up Ravi. Ravi is also shaken. His veneer has fallen. He looks mortal, weak. She does feel sorry.

-   Ravi I am leaving

Her voice starts trembling. She grasps her dress. To be still, calm.

-   Where are you going?
-   I will be gone
-   Are you mad sweetie
-   This is better dear.

She hangs up hurriedly. She fears becoming weak. Its not easy leaving. She thinks of ma. She thinks herself selfish. But no other choice. The knot is silky. Vibgyor dopatta touches neck. Like a warm hug. She closes her eyes.

Ravi can't sleep anymore. Lata's call is disturbing. Hard days taught him. He is in love. Ravi dials Lata's number. Will he call police? The consequences frighten him. He calls up Jai. The humbug switched off. He will thrash him. Restless, he calls police.

IV

Early mornings are cool. HE always strolls now. This is HIS duty. HE reaches in time. HE stays with them. Even before the time. This morning is fresh. The rainbow is perfect. HE loves picture as well. HE pans HIS frames. The boy is restless. He pants and puffs. He loves a girl. HE looks at her. She looks so radiant. Emotions recollected in peace. HE can't squander love. HE remembers HIS girl. HE took her away. That sin pegged HIM. When can HE stop? HE doesn't know yet. But HE leaves her. The boy comes in. Welcome HE says him. Then lifts and leaves.

Trinity

Moon hides

Your eyes

Pour Sun

It goes without saying that we all want to look our best today. You need
to look slim and radiant.

You have overeaten probably and you look so insecure in the Benarasi.

I advised you to drink plenty of water and juices.

In my house I am very particular about shape and fitness and I expect
everyone in my house to follow.

Did you follow? I am unsure, your skin looks dehydrated.

You cannot deceive my eyes – you have not exfoliated your neck, arms or
your upper back.

You forgot that you have to maintain your skin – silky and smooth.

And what an ugly hairdo.

I had known since the beginning, your mom has low taste. She can't
match me.

What did you save on – money?

But you lose my trust.

I couldn't concentrate on the lens.

As the makeup man's hand wriggled over her hand drawing a snake I felt slippery.

I wanted to play on her hands lean yet roundish and pale.

Her long fingers and shapely nails invite me to bury my face in them.

She would have held my curly hair and draw me closer. I was almost about to stumble on her as I leant forward.

She looked up and smiled. Did I expect a wink? The girls of the other world might have.

But she is class conscious. I hate their mentality of ignoring us.

I know how far they can go – in park, in cheap hotels, during the pujas. But not beyond, none.

I wish I could rip off most of them. Till they are tattered into pieces like the confetti of birthday parties.

Somehow I can't get angry with her. Her discomfort in the virgin dress and the overwhelming makeup makes her look so cute.

I wished I can take her to the anti-room and relieved her from her burden.

Decades follow centuries

In sly forgetfulness, and

I gather the dust of collective memory –

Yours, mine and the children of loveless languor.

You have small eyes.

He always dote your eyes – perky, he told me first time.

But now they look so mundane, like the eyes of a dead fish.

Maskara uplifts the eyes – gives them a deeper look.

But one needs to know how to apply.

Black eyeliner is a misfit for your eyes. You should have used a softer

shade.

Take a photo and you know how dull you look.

A camera is less forgiving than a mirror.

Lips!

Your lip liner outline is not even and much darker than your lipstick.

Also, the outline should have been filled with extra layer of long-wearing

matte colour.

Thin and small lips look more sensuous with light lip colors.

You should know deep colours don't suite you, looks really gawky.

As I drew close to her face intently trying to capture every bit of emotion the doors to a secret longing ruptured open.

I can see me with her in the bath softened with rose petals.

She is naïve and firm and I so longed to hold her in my hands – her taut breasts coy and playful.

I move closer to her taking her in my arms and lifting to the side of the bath.

We lay there still, clasping our hands and I can hear my hear beat. Does she hear mine?

I was ashamed. I was ashamed if she heard my longing beating away so heavily.

She pulled her up and looked intently at me – 'You love me?' she asked.

I was in two minds.

I have yearned for her for so long.

From the corner of the street as I looked out at her house – the long dark glasses and the sentry to ward off people like us.

And I could see her face perched against the window of her car and have thought how she would look like.

Naked.

And without makeup.

For so many days I thought how round her breasts would be and her tapering waist.

Her triangle of love is what she sacredly saved from us.

I wanted to feel her, inch by inch - the textures of a rich virgin.

I have long hung up my lens for her.

I lost you at dawn,

When the trains wake up, and

I pray never to follow

That arrow - in your eyes

Mehendi.

The fragrance.

The darker the mehendi colours the intense gelling you will have with me.

Red is the colour.

The golden designs fill up nice.

The wedding couple and the baraat on your hand look pristine.

The lemon and honey application makes it look so fresh.

Someone said more honey you might have put, the sweeter will be

behaviour. Superstitions.

I know you will stay aloof.

You will wait for the mehendi to disappear.

She repeated her juvenile question.

I never believed in love. I never afforded to.

I believed in pumping hard – my emotions, my bike and my girl.

So I kept still.

She moved down and lay her head on my bare chest.

I felt like Shahrukh.

Her ear-rings poked and I was uncomfortable.

The smell of her hair was alluring and her dark tresses were long and captivating.

'You only want to have my body, right?' she asked softly.

I didn't answer.

'My brother was a driver of your father. One of the many' I was surprised I spoke.

'Is it? What was his name? I never knew' she seemed innocent.

'What's the use? When your father's assistant ran over a pavement dweller because they were having something then and there in the car, the police took my brother to jail' the words came out of my mouth like the first trams in the morning – as if they had no past or future.

'Your father promised him, if he posed as the driver of the car then he will get money from your father. My brother was never told the man actually died after being run over'.

I could see her pout lips swell up and her eyes lowered on to her mehendi – the baraat, the couple, elephants and the holy war.

No-man's land

I

Just where the river bends away there is a light. It is on the wasteland where there was sugarcane and vegetables grown regularly. Probably even 10 years ago as well. Now the river dried up along with the one inside the people on both sides of it. It is 5 AM and quite dark with the winter chill. Time stands still. The light, from few torches, becomes visible now. The Border Security Force *jawans* are coming, their heavy boots marking the soft mud of this waste-land.

- 'Where is he?' asks the leader impatiently
- 'Somewhere here only, I guess. He cannot hide. The villagers saw him near stone pillar 2100 last night' a second voice is heard
- 'The forest officials should have told us earlier. Its already more than four hours' the leader is irritated.

It is almost a month that there is no event in his area. He patrols stone pillars designated for him with his troop. Yet there is nothing that happens. Watching the children play football is the only entertainment. Even the red-lantern girls are monotonous, repetitive, demanding. How he wished to plunder the villages of the other side at gun-point – for adventure if not anything. But the High Command ordered – to keep peace.

He is Milan, the leader.

The other two *jawans* are flashing torches occasionally and at random. When suddenly there is a shot. A bullet ripping the fabric of a moist, shy dawn – the flutter of birds and then there is again, a slumber. The villagers are too accustomed to this. But Milan feels his blood starting to get warm.

- 'What are they doing?' a junior asks. He is new here.
- 'Probably just flexing fingers!' Milan gets gawky, 'they don't even get the sluts I guess' his loud laughter breaks the last tinge of peace that lingered on this part of the world.

The Sun breaks out. It is serene. Green.

II

- 'I don't want to hear anything Milan. I have told you long back. Even now there is no trace of Shiva? Are you kidding me?' the forest official knows business
- 'Sir, actually, we couldn't find him anywhere. He can be seen from anywhere isn't it? But he just disappeared', Milan pleads.
- 'No Milan. I don't believe you. Have you asked the Rifles? He might have gone there as well. Who knows?'

Milan dislikes this part most. He knew this will come up again. He doesn't like talking to Rahman – the leader of the Rifles. 'Behenchot' Milan would refer him as.

- 'Rahman', shouts Milan
- 'Whats up?' the reply is sharp.
- 'Shiva is missing. Has he entered your land?' Milan tries to keep the conversation economical.
- 'Yes. And we have hold him captive' Rahman laughs showing is yellow teeth, 'he is in love with our Salma. Wait, he will be given a lesson this time'
- 'Don't you dare Rahman. There will be bloodbath this time. I am too hungry for long' sneers Milan.
- '*Arre, jah jah*. Will see. Now run to your officers and tell.' Rahman turns round.

III

Shiva waits in the open field. This is where Salma used to stand and look at him. So many times when he practiced on the opposite side he saw her looking at him. Her coy smile seduced him to wilderness. He signaled at her, and she would reciprocate. He is bore with loading the trucks with timber. He is in love. He never understood human beings. Did they ever understand him? How could they possibly keep him captive away from Salma. He knows they have kept Salma under watch as well. Shiva grunts loud.

- 'Na Rahman. We can't do this. We have to return him to India. The strict directive that I got is, we are now having peace with India. So

Bangladesh Rifles will show them that. Anyway I heard you fired in the morning?' a senior officer inquires

- 'Janab,that's nothing serious. Just to trap the elephant, sir' Rahman explains.
- 'Ok, now settle it with that guy, whatever his name is. I want this elephant to return to India by today. Inter-religion relation we won't tolerate' the officer thumps.

IV

The barbwire on this stretch is arranged such that the tempos carrying fish across the border do not have any problem. The fences remain open from both sides till noon. All the exchanges happen then. The night ferries them who are not to be seen in daylight. Rahman plunges the dart on Shiva's caudal rump. It's longer than the hand injections but Rahman does not want to take chances. But he is always rough and wild – in a fit he jabs hard at Shiva. Shiva grunts out loud as the narcotic drips in his vein. There is a deep wound but Rahman guesses by *that* time Shiva will be with the *jawans*. 'Who cares then?', he laughs. He opens the fence and kicks Shiva – 'Go'.

Shiva is confused. The effect of narcotic mingles with the soft breeze. The wound has ceased to bleed. He wants Salma to caress him now, to heal his wounds. The other fence opens. Shiva sees Milan and a few others. He does not want to go back. He wants Salma and he turns.

It isn't easy to go back. None of the going backs ever are. Here it's simple for humans to negotiate the fencing. Not for Shiva. The wires of the fence cut his trunk in places. Shiva exercises his weight on the fence. Rahman did not expect this. He wanted to make Shiva incapable of work by applying high dose of narcotics. After all it is an Indian elephant!

V

- 'Who said you to fire?', the officer glares
- '*Janab*, he was trampling our border', Rahman tries to reason.
- 'And what poison did you give him. You thought no one will notice that? India is going to make a big issue with this, you know. Dumb soldier!'
- '*Janab*, he would have killed us if I waited. We can charge it as a terrorist attempt. Believe me'
- 'That's because you silly poisoned him. It took so long for our leadership to work for peace with India. Now, with dumbasses like you all efforts go down the drain. And, I am not sure if we can charge an elephant as terrorist', the senior official gets frustrated.

Milan oils his rifle. It is quite long that the barrel remained cold. He has negotiated with Bangladesh Rifles – bullet for bullet. There won't be any escalations to the higher officials. 'Let us settle it amongst us *Miyan*. I have some good customers for the tusk and the rest. We can have double. Don't you worry, I will manage our side. The elephant got mad and so no other choice – I will tell this. You also tell the same' he suggested the Rifle's officer.

It is quite dark now. But not that dark to miss Shiva's huge body lying on a side. In this light darkness, another shadow comes in. Rahman guides Salma out of the fence, pats her ears and fondles her trunk a last time.

Milan kneels down and aims. Bullet for a bullet is the deal.

VI

The villages throng in numbers. Its long they haven't seen such a show. Two of the giant elephants lying in blood and flesh – massacred and ravaged. The forest officials on both sides have gathered too. They have done an initial investigation. The anti-terrorist squads are believed to be on the way. The order is yet to come as to how the case will be handled jointly – by Bangladesh and India.

The place of the terror is a strip of land - the No-man's land.

Reverence

Sita gets impatient. She has been waiting outside this temporary makeshift clinic for almost an hour now. There are almost ten girls like her there. She just leans her head back against the bamboo frame. The temperature suddenly got low since last Saturday. She remembers she was waiting for Ramu, her brother. Ramu works in the city mill. He was returning from work after almost three months. He brings in hope, and warm clothes.

-'Sita Naskar. Who amongst you is Sita?' shouts the matron when Sita awakes from her rumination.

-'Lie down there, on that bed and lower your salwar. And the pants too', the doctor is nonchalant.

Sita is shy. She has never bared her like this in front of a man. But only once.. she sighed.

-'Fast, fast. We have to test the other girls also and then in the next village' the matron is irritated. Understandably so, she will have to return home in the city by evening. Sita closes her eyes and lies down on the bed.

She can feel the filth, the dry passage of subconscious agony mixed in the stains of pubic blood. She is fifteen only. May be a month or two more. Ma used to tell her about city. The lights of the city. Ma loved red as a colour and Sita remembers how she was so confused and panicked at her first blood. Blood is always red she thought earlier. Last Saturday she felt blood is black too. Sticky and black. So much that it won't go, it won't leave its mark even after she washed repeatedly. She was hysteric. Ma is no more to comfort. There is no one else. Sita sometimes thinks, is this every woman's fate, she is alone, her Ma is also alone – in the city. She never comes home. Sita knows why, she doesn't question that anymore now.

The doctor stoops on her vagina with a pair of tongs and scissors. There are so many things on the tray. Sita gets afraid. She prefers to close her eyes.

- 'Hmm. Do you feel pain?' The doctor inserts something inside her and Sita instantly knows that she can't bear it any more.
- 'Leave me sir. I know what happened. I am telling' Sita reasons.
- 'No. The political cadres will do so. They will help you. But I have to prepare a detailed report. Okay?' The doctor goes back at pricking Sita's private parts.

The mornings are the best time for Sita. She gets up early and goes to the river bed. With Malati and Latika she collects snails and shells. Its fun. Also that is the time for their girly talks as well. Sita is worried that Madan is taking interest in Malati. Madan is a drunkard. Malati is too simple, Sita gets angry with her only. 'See, that Madan is only after your body. He doesn't love you, you know?' Sita said. 'How come you so sure? He has promised me a sari.' Malati basks in glory. Latika is the news supplier for them since her father is close to the Panchayet leader's driver.

The doctor finishes his part. The matron, as sombre as she can be, draws a piece of cotton and throws at Sita,

- 'Clean yourself, for God's sake' she is impatient.

- 'See, your case is confirmed. Multiple occurrences. This is my part, rest your political leaders in Panchayet will do. Don't ask anything from me' the doctor washes off the blood in his hands.

Malati gets in next and Sita decides to wait for her. This is the first time Latika is not with them. She is 'saved'. Its such a strange feeling when you are not in the same group where you belonged. You are now part of this new group – of 10 teenage girls.

Latika told them that police and security forces will be coming to their village - 'Baba is worried. He said, they will beat all of us and take away the land.' Sita wasn't convinced, 'Don't be afraid silly. Its not easy, you know. Our Panchayet is here. They will save us. Its our land, if we don't give how can anyone take that?'

The next day they heard it in the market as well. No one knew what is going to happen, police is fine but what is security force? Whose security are they ensuring? Sita couldn't sleep that night. She sent message to Ramu for coming home. Dada is the only one who loves her. She knows that. She also knew that she is afraid.

Malati is all tears. Sita also feels like crying but seeing Malati cry she decides to stay firm. She feels sorry for Malati. She is such a kid. They heard, Madan has gone missing since Saturday. Is she crying for her or for losing Madan? Sita is unsure.

- 'Girls. Come here. These babus have come here to investigate. They will send reports and the Government will help all of us', the political cadre tries to comfort.
- 'Sir, both these girls were there that night. Sita, you tell how many persons were there?'
- 'How did it start? Don't hide. This is required for their report.'
- 'They took you near the farmhouse of the Ghosals'. Right? What were you wearing?'
- 'Did they take off all your clothes? Or did they tie your hands and mouth?'
- 'How many persons? All at once or one by one?'
- 'See, we need to ensure that such atrocities against women don't occur again. So that you don't have to face this again, or any other girl of the village.'

The questions start bombarding them as if they are peeled off each layer of vanity. The lips moistened, saliva moving all over the crooked faces. In broad daylight, without moving an inch, they raped Sita.
Sita knew this would happen. Every detail will be plundered like the last thread from her body. That night was only for an hour. This day is for hours, this month is for days, this year is for months – on and on and on, the chronicle of rape.

Sita has thought it many times afterwards. What is in it for which this has become such a big farce? Latika told how her sister is raped every night by her brother-in-law. But is it that there is no pain in it? Can rape be classified – graceful rape or not? She laughs. She knows, Ma is raped every night. She knows Ma loved only one man. She knows a lot, which is Sita's problem.

In the middle of long chilly nights Sita wondered the definition of dignified woman. Ramu was upset and wanted to take her with him. But Sita knows that dada lives with friends in a mess, he cannot take her there. He will have to rent a new place and that will be too costly. 'Can't we girls take our own decision ever? Why should we always depend on men?' Sita asked Ramu. Ramu doesn't have answers to any philosophical questions ever, he knows he has to earn a lot for himself, to marry off her sister.

In the midst of the market Sita felt lost. She has come alone from her village. There is only one bus from there in the morning. Latika has pleaded not to leave, 'What will you do there Sita? And what you mean by reverence?' Sita also doesn't know what she means, she spent the whole night thinking of it and she took this decision. Spending more time with Latika means Sita will lose her stance. Latika has an infectious nature. She may force Sita to change her decision. But now that she is already in the city, she feels a little insecure. She has that doctor's name and address, she also took direction of his chamber. But now as she stands near the chamber she feels nervous. Is the decision good? Or may be leading Malati's life was better. Even Ma's. Ma atleast has Sita. What will Sita have?

- 'Hmm. So why did you come here? I cannot give any false reports now. If you wished I would have saved you from this dis-honour, then. Poor girl.', the doctor's eyes lit up as if he found his prey in his den
- 'No Sir. I have not come for that' Sita clears her throat, 'I have come for a little bit of reverence, for me. I will pay you all the charges and your fees. But you have to operate. You have to remove my ovaries. I don't need them. And no one else also should need them.'

The sun is at its furthest. The occasional mild wind makes the pleasant weather waver a little, reminds everyone of the merciless nights. Sita wraps the shawl tightly. She has won the first battle, and she knows that this time she is right.

Company

The ambulance rushed through the moon-lapped free-way. Its full moon tonight and she thought she chose the night to perfection. Baba was sitting on her side with his hand on her forehead. Baba was tense. A trickle of water flowed down Mona, as if, followed by a gush and she was sinking.

Blood isn't clotting as Mr.Biswas could sense her daughter slowly slipping away. His daughters – one tied to the other like beads of same flower. He wished the ambulance could fly.

Two decades ago on such a full moon night Sipra, his wife gave birth to them – Mona and Dona. He lost Sipra that night itself. Moon has enmity with him?

Am I afraid? I am not for my own death. HE had lurked for so long – all twenty years of my life. I am afraid with Baba. What will he do? He is so alone. We were the only ones for him. And now that we both will die, can he withstand that shock?

Mona is mad. What does she think of herself? She is the boss? She never was. She is so puritan. Always tying to be diplomatically correct. I have told her so many times that we cannot lead an ordinarily simple life shouldn't prevent us from enjoying it. Who is she to decide

I now think, were there any other alternative? I had been adapting so much for Dona, but at times I also need something for me.

For me alone.

what will I do with my life? Just because I cannot do anything without her doesn't mean that I can't have my wishes. We have separate heads and a separate heart, she forgets.

If she dies what will happen to me? Foolish girl.

An hour back as the family was preparing for dinner Mr. Biswas wanted to have green salad. Onions, he wanted – to be chopped alongside cucumber. If only Mona ever told him what is going on in her mind. She is a timid girl – sensitive and recoiled. Mr. Biswas loves this daughter of his a bit more for being so mild. Dona is arrogant since childhood, a bad mouth always.

Mr. Biswas never could imagine Mona taking the knife in the kitchen and slitting her own neck in a flash. Dona also couldn't resist, Mona was fast.

Now, her beloved daughter is lying in a pool of blood.

I never could accept Ismail. He is an old pervert. We were his objects of desire. How could Dona love him? We have nothing in common – he

Mona is a frigid. She doesn't have any physical sense. She tells me that I am a nympho. I don't care what she feels. I have hated ma for and us. And, Dona should understand that we cannot marry Ismail.

Can we marry any one person like that? Marriage is not destined for us.

And love? I have loved Akshay for so long. But that is always platonic. That is what is possible for us.

Did I disappoint Akshay? May be. But it is better than disappointing myself.

giving me such a cursed life. Baba always loved Mona more. He never loved me. What was my fault?

I hoped they would kill us at birth. Three women should have died during the event of a birth. Only ma could escape, not us.

Mona shies when people mock us. I am not so tender. I felt betrayed, I hated myself all in my life.

Ismail is the only one who could love me. He made me feel like a woman. Complete, with a man.

When Mona and Dona were young they always wanted to hear the story of Janus. He was the 'god of Gods' is what Mr. Biswas always told them. The god who could look at the past and the future, who could look at the rising and the setting suns. Dona always wanted to know what happened to Janus –" How did he die Baba?". "Gods don't die, dear", Mr. Biswas could always get away with Dona.

Mona was more serious – "Why do you call him only Janus? They are two, aren't they Baba, like us?" Mr. Biswas, a middle-class clerk in a Government office spent his life mending the holes in his existential membrane.

He could never answer Mona's queries.

As the ambulance pulled up inside the hospital, the stretcher and the helpers rushed in. Mr. Biswas has a friend who is a doctor here and the supervision will be proper. Mr. Biswas jumped off when Mona clutched the corner of his shirt.

"Baba, I was wrong. Please forgive me", Mona started sobbing.

"Keep quiet Mona, don't be so nervous", Mr. Biswas couldn't hide the tension.

You can not be deprived of your freedom is what I thought always.

What is freedom? And whose?

When Ismail made love to Dona, I was raped. Dona wouldn't listen to me, she was so adamant.

What else can I do? Than to take my life?

Mona doesn't respect my freedom. She isn't aware of hers as well.

I wished she weren't there in my life.

I know she wanted to deprive me of the happiness I have. She wants to destroy herself and she knows she can destroy me thus.

There was a minor operation which had to be done. Mr. Biswas had no choice for his special children. It was grueling. His doctor friend advised – "We are trying our best. You know this isn't a very common case. But dada, more importantly this is a police case and we cannot hide that. Case of attempted suicide and murder in turn".

What the law holds for his daughters, wondered Mr. Biswas. Memories of their growing up came to his mind. It was difficult for him without their mother. And as they grew up, it was more difficult for them. Being girls didn't help either.

As the doors of the Operation Theatre remain closed Mr.Biswas was trying to think what lies in the future without her daughters. He couldn't think of such a life. They filled up so much of his life. For them he let his youth perish in withered wait. Yet he always felt so much stronger than everyone around – being an ideal parent to a couple of less ideal daughters.

But is he tired? He doesn't disallow that. There is so much shame in admitting that. He always wanted everyone to look at the brighter side. Though he knew deep inside, he is tired.

A man tired of repeating the drudgeries of a surrogate life – there aren't any frills, or, excitements. There is only the solitary routine to be carried out – day out and night in.

Its dawn. Mr. Biswas just stepped out of the hospital building. For a whiff of fresh air. The operation was successful. Both the girls got out of danger. It is an amazingly long night. Mr. Biswas has a feeling of empty stomach. With dawn, there will be light, the start of another journey to nothingness, and, there will be police. He is not sure what they will ask. They may harass him and his daughters, he is afraid. "Can we settle internally?", he pleaded with his doctor friend.

"Dada, these days its not like that. The police will come. I can try to see what we can do here. You may need to negotiate a bit, you know?"

I failed yet again. Am I good for anything? This is the only way to get my freedom.

Dona will never understand that this is a price both of us have to give. I paid the price myself and now it's her time.

I will wait, I need to, for my turn.

I will ask if there is any surgery to separate us. Baba told that it's life threatening. As if, there is no threat now, at-least after what has happened.

He will always take Mona's side, I know.

I will ask the doctor to do surgery. Mona needs to agree, she can't deny just because she is weaker than me.

I cannot wait any further, to get my own body on my own soul.

The police inspector was cordial. He didn't want a miscarriage of justice, he told Mr. Biswas. Dona shouldn't get punished for Mona's crime. "Take them home, Mr Biswas, but keep an eye on them. The next time might be too late. I cannot hush it up for your favour also, maybe", the inspector said while counting the raw notes with his finger dripping with saliva.

Mr. Biswas wonders – his two daughters have become enemies. Between dawn and dusk, they will never be friends. He is certain he may need to visit the hospital again.

Till then he will try to give his daughters a good company.

The city never sleeps

The city wakes up. The Point of View of the reader finds an over-bridge. More focus. A huddle of men – aged and young. The PoV advances and we find a young boy in a pool of blood lying on the street.

A speeding bus left its trail in the morning Sun. The boy is dead.

Kamala knows that Gopal is her weakest child. But what else can she do? After her husband left her with three children, she became harsh. Mini, her daughter works as a maid in the sky scrapper. Sibu, eldest among Mini and Gopal loved to play cricket. Every day he would get up early and go to the park to see boys of his age gleam in spotless white uniform. Last winter it was foggy, the protégé of the locality hit a six which flew out of the park. Sibu knew he could catch the ball, his heart pounded. What will the instructor say? It was a difficult one to take. Sibu moved back and on the edge of the pavement.

Gopal refuses to go out in the evenings. Since childhood he was a bit shaky. He won't climb the fence of the stadium to get in. He was afraid, he may fall down. The gang of boys taunted him – 'Are you a man?' They will sniff. And jeer. This makes Gopal even tenser.

'I don't like darkness, Ma' Gopal says. Kamala knows it better for so many years.

Its almost 11 in the morning when Raghu, the tea-stall boy calls Sukhbir – ' Chacha, don't you have the court hearing today?' Sukhbir gets up, he has drudged for so many years and still the stigma won't leave him. This means today also he might have to lose half day's job.

On flashback we find a younger Sukhbir appearing before the district judge. We come to know that Sukhbir was a Government employee who lost his job. Sukhbir did plead with the Judge but the Judge was unrelenting.

He drives a scrap collecting van since then. He doesn't like this job. There is a nexus between the illegal constructors and the security companies of these huge apartment complexes. He takes his van late at night to the sites when a group of teenaged ruffians put scrap – iron and steel on his van. Sukhbir then drives to a deserted factory shed and unloads the van. He doesn't know what happens after, but he guesses that this is illegal.

But does he have a choice? His case is pending in the court and he cannot leave, the police won't allow him to go back to his family.

Gopal loves Sibu more than himself. He knows Dada also loved him more than anyone. Gopal can close his eyes even now and see dada's stiff body. Gopal knew Dada was a die-hard cricket fan. Someone said he did catch the ball before being hit, others don't agree. For Gopal it's the same – he knows Dada missed the catch!

Sukhbir is not happy with the lawyer. 'Sir, I am paying for so many days. Please tell me, don't I have a chance?' The lawyer has seen these cases for many years, and he knows how to milk his clients – 'Wait for another term. Problem is, there are no eye-witnesses for you'.
Sukhbir has been hearing this same reason over and over again. He is fed up. The lawyer gives a wry smile – 'Go to a temple. God can save you'.

Gopal doesn't like his colleagues. They always share lewd jokes, about the girls in the colony. Ravi is the filthiest always discussing about girls' bosom. He passed comments about Mini once. Gopal warned him. 'What will you do, 1cent?' Ravi said. They used to call Gopal '1 cent' – of no use. The others hurled abuses which all ended up with ascertaining that Gopal is a nut.

Sukhbir doesn't feel like going to the temple. He has been there number of times for the last 2 years. He doesn't wish to bribe God again. He enters the chamber of the astrologer whom Meena, Sukhbir's paramour recommended.

'Look bhai, yours case is complicated. Saturn is not in its preferred position. You need to spend a bit to get out of this state', the man smiles scrumptiously. Sukhbir cannot afford that expense. His future is bleak, but there is something in the tone of the astrologer that he doesn't like. There is a threat very near, he is not sure of the astrologer, can he be believed?

Kamala got some food today from the house she works in. They had a marriage ceremony; Kamala was busy with the family for the last few days. They are kind to Kamala, stood by her in her crisis. Gopal is elated, he loves mutton biriyani, and he has seen that Ma has brought aplenty.

Outside Pintu calls him – they have to reach early tonight. Saif is ill and they are less in number. 'You have to be a receiver today', Pintu says. 'Me? I have never been up there? It doesn't stand still', Gopal reasons. 'You and your fake cries, do as told', their leader intervenes. 'It moves sir, I am afraid' Gopal is all tears. 'You rot and your family rots. Give Mini to us, she will earn more than your shit' Ravi shouts and others join him at laughter.

Sukhbir is distraught. He doesn't want to get into a tangle again. As the night progresses, this fear of

unknown hits him high. He gulps few shots of country
liquor. The site today is lighted. He positions the van
besides the scrap yard when suddenly there is sound of a
bomb. He has heard that the political cadres are eyeing
for a share. Is it them? He doesn't know. At the far gate
he can see a mob running towards him. Is this the threat
he is trying to shy away from? 'Flee' someone shouts.
One of those teenaged thugs? He doesn't know. He puts
on the reverse gear and accelerates; the van suddenly
jerks back in a throttle and hits the rear wall. There is a
loud noise and a shout.

Gopal can't take it any more. He can see it coming up, and slowing down. He has to climb up and collect the materials thrown by others who are below. He has never ever done this but he has to prove these thugs wrong. Gopal holds on to the side rail above the wheel and he hears the sound of a bomb.

The city has gone to sleep. The fluorescent lamps have
created an illusion. There are occasional screeching
sounds from the brakes of some drunken truck drivers.
The frame moves and holds a wall – juxtaposed with
slogans of political parties and occasional sex therapy
advertisements. Besides, a boy lies. The boy is dead.

The Red Lantern

The red lantern is fighting its last breath. No, its not windy. Its just that its life is no more. Its well past 1 at night. The lust of the night is lull now. He waits in the lawn, hundred meters away. The sky above is studded with jewels. He can still find the ones he wanted as a child – wanted and forgot. Many of his friends could reach up and get them – not him. Alas, he sighed heavily.

Somewhere near the old church clock shuddered the time as he turns – the lantern is dead.

Peeing in public toilets is so intimidating for him. Almost always he feels someone might be looking over from the next slot. He is rather unsure. Is he ok? Or is he small? There are no friends to consult. When he grew up in school everyone jeered at him. 'Shorty' was the name he got. What else can he do? He used to hang from trees – an advice someone gave him or his mother. Nothing happened. He only fell and broke his hand. His mom cursed herself – 'You didn't get my milk. That's why you are like this'. He knew that his mother had an infection when he was inside her. Is it the reason? May be. Maybe not. His mother is happy atleast to assign it to some reason. That keeps her satisfied, he thinks.

She is taut. He had desired her so many times. He almost felt her round breasts whenever he thought of her. She was a hit. She never had to be on the street. He was one of them who used to find a client for her. There were two more. He didn't like the job. Not for her atleast. The other two used to be with some other girls of the area. And he knows they also yearned for her. But he couldn't be with anyone. How can he do so? 'You Shorty. No girl will ever take you' they rebuked. He knew at heart that it was true. But money can buy almost everything. He knew that as well. But he doesn't have money to waste on useless girls. Can love be bought with money? Novels say you cannot. He is not sure.

He loved talking to her. She was good to him. At times she would give him good cigarettes, left by her clients. He was shy. The other guys would laugh at her. 'You are harmless Shorty. That's why she talks to you so much.' Whatever it is, he was happy. The shanty where he was staying with his mother is a little walking distance. When he returns almost at dawn he would see his mother sleeping while sitting. 'Don't wait for me, ma' he told many times. The old woman won't listen. She knows his son is too soft to survive this cruel world.

'Drink milk' said the sadhu, 'and you will grow. Every human drinks milk to grow up.' He was confused. He loves drinking milk. 'You have to drink milk from a woman who is having milk. This is what you lacked. Cow milk will not help.' The idea seemed absurd. Where will he get such a woman? And why will she agree? 'Any other alternative? Which is easier?' he asked. 'Easy alternatives don't help if the problem is difficult, beta. But still you can hold this stone for a month and see if it helps. There may be a chance. Check, if you wish', the sadhu had told. He is wearing the ring since then.

He is certain there are no improvements. On the contrary he is having stomac problems since then. He doesn't understand planets but his mother was certain 'This new ring is causing all the problems. See, you haven't earned much as well in the last few months. Throw it away'. He couldn't throw away the ring. Its not his type to be so assertive. But its true that for the last few months his earning is low.

She was in love with one of her clients — the school teacher from the city. The man is perfect, good match — he always thought looking at them together. Problem started few months ago. There were rumours even before but he never knew what it was all about. He was shy to ask as well. She was pregnant. He knew it was that man only. One day she called him and handed over a letter 'Give it to the schoolteacher. He will be in the ferry-ghat'. So he acted as the messenger. One day when he came to work she had left. She eloped pregnant. No one had a trace. He knew she had fled with the schoolteacher. They all pounced on him for information, they all knew he might know something. But he didn't tell a thing — not even that the schoolteacher plans to marry her and settle in the big city. No one can find her ever he thought. He was pensive that he couldn't see her again but she was secretly happy. This is a hell. He will be happy if she can raise her child away from here.

Nature has its own way of judging things. Time changes colours to everything, to minds of people as well. He got accustomed to working for newer girls. When suddenly one day he finds she is back. She is pale and anemic with a son. The owner was good-hearted to take her back though she may take a while to be back on trade. 'But you need to be taken to doctor for checkup', he advised. 'I know but I don't have any money. That bugger took everything from me' she started crying. He didn't want to hear the story. Its an old story. It repeats with perfection. He somehow felt annoyed.

As the night grew old and the clouds moved faster across the ceiling of his thoughts he felt a desire to be at her side. She is a friend to me, he thought. He knew she is very helpless now, more than before and he is her only friend as well. 'I will take you to the doctor' he announced the next day. 'But why? Why will you spend your money? I will be on trade from next month and will go myself' she reasoned. She couldn't keep up to it. Two days later she fainted. He took her to the doctor. 'Nourishment is missing. She has to eat well' the doctor prescribed along with few medicines. 'Thank you. You are a friend. I always knew you are. But what can I do in return?' she was coy. 'Nothing. That you acknowledge me as a friend is more than what I want. I always secretly admired you. But couldn't tell you' he gasped. That he could tell all these he never could believe. ' I like you too. You were different from most. You were so natural. So obvious' she burst into words that flowed over the both of them as they swayed in momentary happiness. The black clouds move away from the face of the moon and in his exuberance he says 'The sadhu baba told me to drink milk from a woman. I will be a normal man then. Not a shorty any more. Will you let me? When I become normal then we can have a future'. There are words which remain best never uttered. She was frozen. He overlooked in his new found energy and prospect. 'Okay, come to my room when you are done with your work. I will wait', she could utter hiding her tears.

Suddenly the lights get dim and in silhouette we find the seven of them – hand in hand gliding over the land. The music is sombre, from a harp supported with violin. He enters her room – its lighted beyond imagination. She lies there – calm and still. There is nothing on her. He could see her naked body for the first time. So silken and white. So full and curvy. He could almost touch her from trance. There was only a piece of cloth round her neck – like the royal scarf she is wearing. Transcendence from the trivial, he felt perplexed and overawed. He never believed that his destiny would come to here. He walks to the lawn. Lies down as if the sky is so near. The atmosphere is still, yet the red lantern dies its death. He looks at it – 'Poor soul', he pities it. There was a bird in him which fluttered very recently. He then lets her fly away.

As the screen gets opaque we can hear in voice-over a chanting that fades with the opening lights of the dawn -

"Emperor, your sword won't help you out

Sceptre and crown are worthless here

I've taken you by the hand

For you must come to my dance"

Priapism

I

The doctor pulls out a big syringe. He fills it up with some fluid. Ravi is nervous. Will this work? Is it a good decision to come here? His friend Samir suggested this place – cheap and effective.

- 'Don't get afraid. You will have a big one for sure', the doctor quips seeing Ravi sweating up.
- 'Is it just one time doc?' Ravi is anxious
- 'Yes, this one is one time. Seeing you reaction I will prescribe a course of 2 months. Then who can stop you? You will be like a horse' the coarse teeth of the doctor are visible for a few seconds.

The doctor asks him to lie down and pushes the needle. A sharp surge of piercing sting makes Ravi shiver, he almost faints.

- 'Lie down lucky man. After 10 mins get onto your own and explore and invade. Plunder what you are gifted with', the doctor sneers.

He was the dumbo of the group. Friends would take money from his pocket and eat icecreams. Later on they would force him to buy Debonair. 'What will you do seeing these girls even' they would say. 'You will get good decent girls, leave these to us', Samir would jibe at him. If only he can teach them a lesson.

II

Its quite dark now. The frame is occasionally lit up by the flickers of a lonely street light. Soon the eyes of the viewer get adjusted to the opaque stillness of a winter light. The camera finds Ravi loitering outside a dilapidated one-storied building. This one is one of the many such in this part of the city. A man stoops on Ravi from the dark alley,

- 'Babu, what are you looking for?' he smiles
- 'How much?' Ravi can feel the heat
- 'Depends. Good College piece will cost more. Try one babu', the predator closes onto his prey.

Ravi nods and follows his pied-piper. There is no sound apart from the dry squeaking of the old leaves being trampled. The sound slowly increases in a staccato and compounds into a thundering squelch – a woman cries.

The black screen is torn apart by a lightning which is punctuated with the woman's scream.

III

Kalpana looks at her watch. Its nine. Her accomplice confirmed that the man has still not been out. Its over half hour now. Kalpana knows men don't survive that long. She gets little fidgety. It's a rainy night. How long will she be on the prowl? But this is her job. A job she has taken herself.

This case would have been quite straight-forward. The customary back-ground check was polka-dotted but that is ok. She found out that in most of such cases these dots vanish with time, they are not bothersome. She prepared her report and the evidences, documents – everything is ready.

Just one bit when yesterday her assistant found the man in one of those quack's clinics.

IV

Ravi looks at the torso of the pale girl. Poor soul, he thinks. She is still wriggling in pain, quite understandably as well.

- 'Are you a man or a beast?' she seethes. Ravi keeps quite.
- 'You are so rough. No one has undone me like this. And you know it pains', she touched her tender insides which felt like a ravaged city of nothingness.

He was surprised. It started well and he was happy that the medicine worked. He had a huge turn on and he couldn't believe he can be so manly. The girl who introduced herself as Rimi was coy and she was apprehensive. He promised to be gentle,

- 'You will have to teach me. You drive' he reasoned. She didn't believe him. But he knew what he said.

Yet, he couldn't control. The face of Dipa, his childhood muse came up so many times – she rejected him like a sanitary towel.

V

Kalpana reaches for her mobile. Its on vibration. Kumar, his accomplice gives a missed call. That's what is planned. That means the man is coming out. Kalpana quickly looks up the small mirror from her purse, just a tad of the lip gloss – red. She unbuttons the shirt a bit, her round breasts swell to the cold air that blows past them. She spots him round the lane as she speeds up

- 'Oye' she hisses. He seems to be in a hurry. Kalpana follows him and holds his hand back.
- 'What hero? Don't like me darling?', she bends forward a little. The men don't refuse her curves, she knows. Only Sanjay refused her, refused her to this point. She gets pensive for a while but she knows she has to do her job first. She will have to hold back her hatred towards men, atleast till she earns a lot.
- 'I have to go, leave me. I am not interested', the man tries to break away.
- 'You are my hero of the night. I won't let you go sir. Its raining and I have not earned a penny. I will satisfy you. Guarantee.' She pleads effortlessly.
- 'I can't pay you much', the man tries to fight his desires.

- 'You don't have to pay for the pimp or the room rent. Take me to your room', Kalpana finds a solution.

The man is in two minds. His carnal desires are far from being satiated. He can still feel the bulge in his pants. He is not relieved. He knows he needs a girl now. But too much money is flowing out tonight. When will this drain stop?

VI

This is now an indoor setting. A bare room insinuated with the trickle of water from the side walls makes it even murkier. She lies on the crumpled bed looking at the man. She has seen so many men behaving so very different ways when it comes to proving their mettle. She feels like laughing loud – poor men, their all intelligence and prowess is confined only to this small head.
She moves a bit,

- 'What do you do, sir' she tries to be innocent
- 'I do business. Whats your name?', the man questions
- 'I am Dipa. Your name sir?' She quips.
- 'What? You cannot be Dipa', the man suddenly flared.
- 'Ok sir, if you wish you can call me Meeta' she knows these are lies – black or white is beyond her comprehension.
- 'I am Rakesh' the man hesitates.
- 'Are you married Rakesh?' Meeta asks.

- 'No. But I will be shortly. What do you think of me, will I be a good player?' Rakesh chuckles
- 'You will be great sir, any girl will be privileged to get you. But why couldn't you wait, if you are getting married soon?' Meeta rubs herself onto his hairy chest. Rakesh springs like a wounded leopard
- 'Cause I have to find out. If I can do it' he shouts, 'all the girls used to tell I am impotent, that I will never ever satisfy a girl. Now look at me, look at me. I can rip you off into two. You and any girl.'
- 'You will hurt me sir' Meeta seems a little nervous. Is there a twist in the tale?
- 'Yes I will. And I will make you beg for help.' Rakesh just goes overboard.
- 'No Sir. Leave me then. And don't marry', Meeta gets up and tries to move away.
- 'NO. Don't ever try to run away. I have paid you to obey my orders' Rakesh suddenly feels as if he is royal, the blood boils. The blood has been boiling for many hours now and there are no signs of cooling.

VII

Kalpana senses that there is a problem. This man is not the type she thought of. He is betrayed, but his actions will be dangerous. He can rape any girl with his killer instinct. She tries to pacify this man but he isn't. The strange erection of the man confuses her even more. How can he remain like this? What is his source of sensation? He talks about some injection; the quack must have administered some illegal drug which makes him so inconsolable.

Kalpana thinks of herself. Is she different from this man? She also lost her love to petty politics and now she is throttling her life in sleepless nights. Is there any decency in this life? And there are so many risks. Majority of her assignments are like this only – background check of prospective grooms.

VIII

Ravi just cannot believe this. The doctor never told him that the effect of the injection will last for so long. Its over six hours now. He still feels an urge to go at a girl but Meeta seems to be disobedient. What if his wife be such as well? No girl ever honoured him for anything. The feeling of defeat started seeping in. He looks at Meeta. She is still clothed. This strikes him hard. He picks up the table knife,

- 'Undress.' He shouts.
- 'No', Meeta is firm.
- 'I will cut you to pieces', Ravi's hands tremble in excitement.
- 'Do what you can, I am leaving' , Meeta turns round

IX

In midshot there is a window. The lights from inside have suddenly blown out and there is a shroud of chilly darkness that covers the space. The background score catches the piercing note of a siren and a police van enters the frame. Kalpana comes out and speaks to the officer. The officer nods at her in affirmation. Seems they know each other previously. He instructs his men and they enter the room. Soon they come out with a body draped in white sheet. They put the body in a van and drove away.

Kalpana looks at the watch. Its past midnight. She lights a cigarette and takes a deep breath. The officer asked to visit the police station tomorrow for a detailed case history. Before that, she needs to catch some sleep.

Appendix

Radha	-	Originally published in *Writing Raw* magazine on January 2010.
18th June	-	Originally published in *Muse India* (ISSN 0975-1815). Last accessed on 15th August 2011 here: http://www.museindia.com/viewarticle.asp?myr=2010&issid=29&id=1860
The four letter word	-	Originally published on June 16, 2010 in *My Little Magazine*. Last accessed on 15th August 2011 here: http://mylittlemagazine.blogspot.com/2010/06/four-letter-word.html
Trinity	-	Originally published in *Sristi*. Last accessed on 15th August 2011 here: http://www.sristi.co.in/SRISTI/SRISTI23/article.php?nick=amitavanag&ar_type=4&ar_name=28
Reverence	-	Originally published on July 17, 2011 in *Woodsmoke*. Last accessed on 15th August 2011 here: http://woodsmoke.wordpress.com/2011/07/17/reverence/
The city never sleeps	-	Originally published in *Indian Ruminations - Journal of Indian English Writers* (ISSN 2249-2062). Last accessed on 15th August 2011 here: http://www.moronicox.com/Priapism-nag.html
The Red Lantern	-	Originally published on May 29, 2010 in *My Little Magazine*. Last accessed on 15th August 2011 here: http://mylittlemagazine.blogspot.com/2010/05/red-lantern.html
Priapism	-	Originally published in *Moronic Ox Literary and cultural journal*. Last accessed on 15th August 2011 here: http://www.moronicox.com/Priapism-nag.html

Zeitfracht Medien GmbH
Ferdinand-Jühlke-Straße 7
99095 Erfurt, Deutschland
produktsicherheit@kolibri360.de

Druck:
CPI Druckdienstleistungen GmbH
im Auftrag der
Zeitfracht Medien GmbH
Ein Unternehmen der Zeitfracht - Gruppe
Ferdinand-Jühlke-Str. 7
99095 Erfurt